BLACK HOLE

RADIO

FURILANI

ANN BIRDGENAW

ILLUSTRATIONS BY NOA NE'EMAN

DFP

Printed in the United States of America

paperback ISBN: 978-1-961624-66-5
ebook ISBN: 978-1-961624-67-2

DartFrog Plus is the hybrid publishing imprint of DartFrog Books, LLC.

301 S. McDowell St.
Suite 125-1625
Charlotte, NC 28204

www.DartFrogBooks.com

I dedicate this book to my family and friends who always spark my imagination.

CONTENTS

CHAPTER 1

ANOTHER EXTRAVAGANZA

"Hawk, Matt, wait up!" We turn around as Big Mikey catches up to us. "Hey, did you guys hear about the science projects?" Mikey shouts as he jumps from foot to foot.

"Not yet. Why?" I ask. Big Mikey and I had been science buddies on the grade six class project. We did a cool project about popcorn. In fact, we had a popcorn party in the clubhouse with the whole basketball team.

"I heard from the other class that Mr. Brain will pick a project from each class to enter into the Regional Science Fair," Mikey continues. "I think he'll pick ours for sure, Hawk." He grins, and we start walking again.

"I don't know about that. Justin and Kelly did a great project about germs in the school, remember?" I look at Matt, and he nods.

"Hey! What about the project Celeste and I did?" Matt asks.

"Mr. Brain is still cleaning cola off the ceiling after you two dropped eighty-eight Mentos into a two-litre bottle of soda and made a cola geyser in the classroom." Mikey chuckles, slapping his forehead. "And no one was impressed when Justin and Kelly said the cafeteria was germier than the boys' bathroom! Eeeww!" Mikey clutches at his throat and gags dramatically.

"Yeah, but that geyser was epic!" I say, as I high-five Matt.

"I still think our project was the best. Everyone loved it!" Mikey says.

"Yeah, because we gave everyone popcorn!" I say, afraid to get my hopes up. Going to the Regional Science Fair would look really good on my report card and my application to space camp.

"If Mr. Brain picks us, we'll have to redo some of the experiments we did at the popcorn party. Oh, maybe we could have another party," says Mikey, rubbing his hands together.

I gulp, thinking of the last time the basketball team came over to Mission Control. That's our UBSS space club—Uranus is the Butt of the Solar System. We tested every kind of popcorn we could think of and created a giant chart: Jiffy pop, microwave popcorn, air-popper, in a pot on top of the stove (with my mom), with coconut oil, butter, yellow corn, white corn, and blue corn. It was a popcorn extravaganza—almost as good as the extravaganza on Bilaluna with the Queen Bee. The team helped us figure out which tasted the best, which was the fluffiest, and which had the highest percentage of popped corn. It turns out if you soak the kernels in water for ten minutes before popping, they turn out perfect. Big Mikey and I were the hosts, and we made sure everyone tried the popcorn and entered their opinions on huge chart paper.

It was all very scientific until Mouse got carried away and stuck a giant popped corn up each nostril. We all fell down laughing until we realized that he couldn't get them out. We were getting a little nervous, but Celeste got the idea to make him sneeze them out. Great idea. But who has a feather when you need it?! So, what else could we do . . . we got the black pepper out. What could go wrong? Poor Mouse choked on pepper fumes and got pepper in his eyes. When he finally sneezed, it was the biggest, baddest sneeze you've ever heard. KaaaaaBlamChheeewww! Whoosh, the popcorn flew out of Mouse's nose like two bullets. That was it; we all fell down laughing again! Even Mouse chortled. I'm not sure, but I think Celeste used her superpower to induce the violent sneeze. We all decided then and there that black pepper-flavoured popcorn was the best new flavour.

And that's when the black hole radio started beeping!

"Hawk," Mikey shouts to get me out of my thoughts, "what do *you* think?"

"Um, I don't think we should get ahead of ourselves, Mikey. Let's find out who is going to regionals first," I say, heading into class.

CHAPTER 2

SCIENCE FICTION FAIR

Friday afternoon in class, Mr. Brain clears his throat and taps his pointer on the board.

"Settle down, everyone. I have a special announcement to make. I have chosen the teams who will participate in the Regional Science Fair next month." He knows we've all been waiting for this announcement. "All the projects were spectacular. Some more spectacular than others, I daresay." He smiles at Matt and Celeste as his eye twitches. "But I can only choose two teams from our school to compete against the other schools. So, without further ado—from my other class, Aria and Madden will present their incredible, air-powered car. From this class . . ." He pauses long enough for all of us to gasp, because we're holding our breath. "Justin and Kelly will present their 'germs in school' project. The school board has changed how they clean and disinfect our schools because of their research and hard work. Well done! You two will make us all proud at Regionals."

Mikey and I make eye contact. We are both disappointed.

After school, on our way to Mission Control, we try to cheer each other up.

"Sorry you and Mikey didn't make it to Regionals, Hawk. I know it meant a lot to you," Matt says as we walk.

"Thanks, Matt. But your project was the bomb, guys! Literally! I never knew Mentos and cola would react like that!" I say.

"Yeah, it would have worked better if the whole package of Mentos didn't fall into the bottle," Matt says, kicking a pebble with his foot.

"But it was so worth it to see all those cliquey girls in class get soaked with cola," says Celeste, tucking her long red hair behind her ear. "I'll never forget the look on Bellamy's face as the sticky brown goo rained down on her perfect blonde head." She quickly looks away. Celeste still has a hard time fitting in with the 'cool' girls in our class.

"I wasn't sure if you had something to do with that, Celeste," Matt says, smiling at her. "The cola came down mostly on their side of the class." He laughs, remembering the shocked cries of the girls as they ran out of class, a wet, brown mess.

Celeste shrugs.

"It's all good. Now we can focus on the basketball city championships. *And* I didn't want to have another popcorn party in Mission Control with Mikey and the team. Remember what happened last time?" I ask, looking at them.

"OMG, it's true! That was a close call!" says Celeste, rubbing her worry stone furiously.

When the radio started beep, beep, beeping at the party, everyone, especially Mikey, noticed. He said, "There's that annoying alarm again, Hawk. Let's turn it off once and for all."

"No!" I shouted and blocked the door to the garage.

"Don't worry about it, Mikey. My dad is bringing all that stuff to Goodwill," I blabbered, as I imagined the whole basketball team transported to some alien planet. I shot Matt and Celeste a 'help me out, here' look.

"Okay everyone, it's time to go home," Matt said, then started herding them toward the exit.

I agreed. "Yeah, my mom said we have to clear out by eight." I put away the bowls and chart paper, hoping they'd get the hint.

Thankfully, Matt and Celeste lured the team outside to throw some hoops in the driveway as I hid the box with the radio. *Whew! How long can I keep this up?*

Mikey hung around to put our science stuff away. "Hey! I know what to do about that beeping sound, Hawk. You should call the Ghostbusters!" He laughed at his joke.

Oh brother! I thought. *More like alien busters!*

"C'mon Mikey, let's go practise and try to win the playoffs! Coach will pee his pants if we make the city championships!"

CHAPTER 3

SPACE JAM

"Basketball is so much fun when you don't lose every game," exclaims Matt, shaking out his wet afro after the game. We walk out to meet Celeste.

"Yeah, we've won ten straight games since Celeste and I joined," I crow, as Matt and I do a little jump and click our space club rings together.

"Coach says we made the final four, and we'll play for the city championships next weekend," boasts Matt.

"I know, right! We just have to beat LCC again, then it's either SSA Academy or Riverview in the final," I add.

"I'm sure it will be SSA Academy. They've won the city championship the last five years in a row," says Matt. "Hey Celeste, wait up!" We run to catch up with her.

"Celeste, you'll have to help us out if we're going to beat them," I worry. Celeste's telekinesis is a key part of our winning strategy. We received special powers from the alien friends we've met when the radio transported us to alien planets. Matt and I have ESP; we can talk to each other in our minds. Celeste has the power to move objects with her brain, which has helped our basketball game a lot.

"I think we're ready," says Celeste shyly. She doesn't like to take credit for our wins.

"Yeah, our team is stronger now, even without Celeste. Mouse sinks baskets from all over the court even after Celeste has left the building," exclaims Matt.

"And if he misses, Stretch jumps up and dunks the rebound," I add, doing a little jump and a swish sound.

"Coach says my lay-up has improved," Matt brags. "Even Mikey is setting me up more often."

"Last practice I noticed that if I hit my sweet spot on the backboard, my hook shot falls right in . . . and with no help from Celeste," I remark.

"Well, I guess we don't need your help anymore," jokes Matt. "Until we play the SSA Bears, that is."

"Gee, thanks Matt!" says Celeste, not laughing.

Then something amazing happens. Bellamy, the 'coolest' girl in school, raises her hand and calls out, "Hey, good luck on the game next weekend! I'll be there to watch." We all turn our heads in surprise as Bellamy just laughs and shakes her head. *Wait, did Bellamy Smith just talk to us? Did she actually wish us luck in the basketball game? Whoa, I think we just became . . . popular*!

***

On the day of the tournament, I get a text from Celeste:

Hawk, I'm sick with the stomach flu. I don't think I can play today.

I type furiously. *What? Are you kidding?* My phone rings, and I answer right away.

"I'm not kidding. I was sick all night," Celeste sobs into the phone.

"Maybe it was something you ate, and you'll be okay in a few hours," I say, unable to accept that Celeste will miss the tournament. *How can we do it without her?*

"I don't think so, Hawk. I can't get out of bed," she cries.

"Can you make it to the gym and help us, even if you can't play?" I plead.

"No, my mom says it's contagious. My dad had it first, and he was sick for three days," moans Celeste.

"What are we going to do? We'll get creamed without you," I fret, running my hands through my blond hair so it sticks straight up.

"You guys will be fine. I haven't helped any of you for the last two games. Just believe in yourselves. Oh, I gotta run, but call me and let me know how it ...." Celeste hangs up before finishing her sentence.

We play one game on Saturday and the second on Sunday, and Celeste misses both games. Matt calls out to me as I leave the gym after the second game.

"Hawk don't leave yet. The coaches are taking us to the mall for sodas to celebrate."

"Okay, I'll be right there. I promised Celeste I'd call her. Order me a cola with milk, will ya?" I say, raising my phone. Matt looks at Bellamy with a grossed-out look on his face but shoots me a thumbs up.

Celeste answers on the first ring. "How did it go?" Not even a hello.

"Celeste, how are you feeling?" I ask first.

"Terrible. You don't want to know. But how was the championship? Tell me, tell me, tell me!" shouts Celeste.

"Guess what? It was amazing. We beat Riverview by 15, and the game with SSA Academy for the championship was a close one. Celeste, we won by one point at the buzzer!" I gush.

"Wow, that's fantastic! Give me all the deets," Celeste says with an exhale of relief.

"We were on fire, Celeste. Stretch scored almost as often as Mouse on rebounds and dunked the ball twice in each game. Matt weaved his way through the key, and Mikey fed him dozens of times for his signature lay-up. It was so great! I focused on my backboard spot, and my hook shot couldn't miss. Mouse, Stretch, Matt, and I were all picked for the all-tournament first team, along with a guard from the SSA Bears. And you won't believe this, but Mouse broke the record for most 3-pointers and was chosen MVP of the tournament." I take a breath.

"Wow, that's so awesome. I knew you could do it! But tell me about winning at the buzzer," pleads Celeste, eager for more details.

"Get this! We were down by one with three seconds left when an SSA guard fouled Mikey as he tried to steal the ball from him. He wasn't shooting, so we got to throw the ball from the side, just inside the SSA zone."

"So, did Mouse throw the final shot?" Celeste jumps in.

"Coach Soggybottom called a time out to work out a play. He had Beaner throw in the ball and told him to either throw it to Mouse for the outside shot or to Mikey so he could pass it to Stretch, Matt, or me. He told Stretch to streak to the left of the basket for an alley-oop, Matt to the right for a lay-up, and me to be outside the key in my hook shot spot." I set up the play for her.

"That's so exciting, Hawk. Which way did it go?" digs Celeste, caught up in the action.

"They double-teamed Mouse, so Beaner threw it to Mikey, who was open. The SSA team played man-to-man, so Stretch, Matt, and I were covered. But Mikey only had two seconds to pass it, and he looked to see who was open and then needed to do something, so he threw up an alley-oop pass to Stretch," I pant and pause.

"And, and?" demands Celeste.

"The guy covering Stretch was in the way, and he couldn't get to the basket. So Matt ran around his man, but he didn't get there right away," I explained.

"So, what happened?" begs Celeste.

"Mikey's pass was right on target, straight over the basket, a perfect alley-oop. But Stretch wasn't there to catch it, so the ball hits the backboard and bounces back at the rim."

"OMG, so it went in anyway?" guesses Celeste.

"The buzzer went off just as it struck the backboard, and when it hit the rim, it looked like it might bounce out, so Matt jumped up to tip it in. But I heard the buzzer and was about to yell 'No' to Matt...."

Celeste interrupts, "Right. If he touched it after the buzzer, the shot wouldn't count."

"Yes, but Matt pulled his hand back just in time. The ball teetered on the rim for a second and then dropped in."

"So, Mikey scored the winning basket. That's so cool!" Celeste gasps.

"Yeah, you should have seen him, Celeste. He was so happy, he jumped up and down, and hugged everyone. Even Bellamy came over and hugged Matt. He turned bright red."

"So Matt must have read your mind?" Celeste says, thinking out loud.

"I never asked him, but I think so," I say.

"Matt should get an assist for not touching the ball," jokes Celeste.

"Yes, and you too, Celeste. The team played harder than ever, and I think they wanted to win it for you. You made us believe we could do it."

CHAPTER 4

GROUND CONTROL TO MAJOR HAWK

I wake up on the orange couch in Mission Control surrounded by Grandpa's journals. I must have dozed off. I still can't believe my grandpa travelled through the black hole radio too! In his logbooks, I read about his adventures in outer space. I thought Matt, Celeste, and I had some crazy adventures on the hyperspace highway, but Grandpa had a lifetime of adventures from Andromeda to the Whirlpool galaxies. Too bad he never shared them with me when he was still alive. Matt and I had to find out the hard way when we got sucked through to planet Shnergla by the beeping radio in a box of Grandpa's old things.

Our last trip was scary because we landed on planet Labyrinthia inside a mammoth underground cave. We had to save ourselves and all the alien-napped child slaves who worked in the mine. What else could we do? We couldn't leave them there. They were so happy when Celeste destroyed the opening of the cave, and the entire top of the mountain collapsed to make sure they couldn't reopen the mine. I still miss Wolfie, though. He's the smart wolf-snow-leopard who helped us, and Kyp too. This reminds me, Kyp gave Matt a shoq-lot crystal as a gift when we left. It's nothing like chocolate—it's what they mined on Labyrinthia. I won-der what it's for. I just read something in Grandpa's

journal about a prism he had. It had enough energy to make things explode! I'd better text Matt.

Dude, did you ever find out what the crystal does?

What crystal?

You know. The crystal Kyp gave you.

Naw. I hid it in my underwear drawer

Bring it to mission control

kk

I text Celeste to meet up at Mission Control for an emergency meeting. We haven't seen her for days, and maybe she can help us figure out what the crystal does.

Matt and Celeste arrive at the clubhouse together.

"It was awesome, Celeste! And then everyone sang; *We are the champions, and we'll keep on fighting till the end.*" Matt starts singing the winner's anthem.

Celeste grins at him, "Cool, Matt! I see you're still wearing your medal."

"Yeah, I showered with it this morning. Ha ha . . . Oh hey, Hawk," says Matt, getting serious when he sees my face.

"Quick! Get in here," I whisper, looking around outside the door to make sure no one is watching.

"What's the emergency?" Celeste asks.

"Shoq-lot." I say

Celeste licks her lips. "I could go for some hot chocolate right now . . . but it's not an emergency."

"I want some too!" Matt jumps in.

"Not that kind of chocolate." I roll my eyes. "Labyrinthia shoq-lot," I say, nodding at the two of them.

Matt puts his hand in his pocket. "Oh right, here it is. But can I still have some hot chocolate?" He shows us the small crystal in the palm of his hand. Suddenly the shoq-lot pulsates and lights up like a tiny flashlight.

"Ayeee! What the . . .?" Matt drops it like it's hot. We all stare at the fading glass crystal on the floor as it blinks a few times and goes out.

"W-What should we do, Hawk?" he whisper-whines. Matt thinks I'm like Stephen Hawking or something, the cosmo-genius I'm named after.

Celeste bends down and puts her finger close to the shoq-lot. It flickers like a lightning bug, then goes out as she pulls her finger back.

"Maybe it's a dilithium crystal? Like in *Star Trekkers!*" says Matt. His eyes are about to pop.

Celeste uses her special power to levitate the alien stone without touching it. The stone tries to light up as Celeste uses her eyes to direct it over to the computer desk, where we can observe it. As she sets it down, the tiny piece of glass shoots out beautiful colours.

"Ooh, it's so pretty. It looks like a rainbow from this side." She runs around the crystal, studying every side. "I think Mr. Brain said a prism can bend the white light to show all the colours of the rainbow. Maybe this crystal is a prism."

"Whatever it is, I think it likes you, Celeste," says Matt watching as Celeste lights it up with her finger, shooting colours out the other side.

"No, Matt. It'll work for you too. Try it," she replies.

As he lights up the prism, I hop on the internet to do some research. I search crystals + energy, and there's tons of information out there. Some crystals can absorb energy from different sources like the sun, uranium, or even a sub-space region of the universe . . . like a black hole! I slap my forehead.

"Hey, you guys. Check this out. It says here that crystals can get their energy from black holes in space. Don't we have a black hole through our radio?" Celeste and Matt look up from the dimly-lit prism.

"What if we put the prism near the radio and see what happens," I say, trying to smile.

"No way, Hawk! That thing is gonna suck us into the wormhole again!" he says, looking at Celeste for backup.

"I don't know, Matt. But this thing is awesome!" Celeste focuses on moving the crystal from one thing to another to see its reaction. "And I could do it with levitation."

"See, Matt. We don't even have to go near it. And we'll see what this crystal can do. Maybe it'll trigger something cool, like our ESP and Celeste's telekinesis," I reassure him.

"What if it's something evil and bad? Remember what Kyp said, powerful enough to blow a planet to bits!" Matt trembles.

"Yes, but only if you put many of them together. It's just a tiny gemstone. A chip, really," I say, jumping up and running toward the garage.

"Wait! I'm n-not ready!" Matt runs behind the orange couch. "Okay, I'm ready."

Celeste approaches the open garage door with the prism in mid-air in front of her. "I'm ready too."

I turn on the light and look for any sign of the radio beeping. "Phew." I take a breath, then creep to the cupboard where we keep the radio and open it. The handbook is next to the radio.

"Here, Matt!" I say, sliding my grandpa's handbook across the floor and through the open garage door. "Check the book to see if there's anything about prisms in it."

Matt crawls on his belly toward the book and flips through it.

"Nope, your grandpa never had to deal with alien crystals or magical prisms," he says, closing the book. "We're on our own here. This is new black hole radio territory."

CHAPTER 5

CHAMELEON SUPERNOVA

The electricity shoots through us. My hair stands on end and my whole body turns into a goosebump. The sparks fly and light flicks around the garage. I look over at Matt and Celeste, but they are blurry and faint, like they are about to disappear. The last thing I remember is the smell of smoke and a loud pop as we all disappear into the radio.

I am lying in a puddle of red liquid when I come to. "Ahhh!" I scream, jumping up and checking myself for bloody injuries. I think I'm okay . . . but the air is thin here, and it takes a while to get used to it. I suck air greedily into my lungs then I gasp. What is that stink? I take a sniff of myself. OMG, I reek! What is that?! I cough and stumble along. *I've been slimed!*

"Matt?" I choke. "Celeste? Where are you guys?"

I notice a small animal watching me from some strange-coloured bushes. At least, I think they're bushes. They're multicolour rainbow plants, and the animal disappears and reappears. I start to walk up the road and notice the creature follows me. When I stop, it stops. When I walk, it walks. If I try to look at it, it blends into the background and disappears like a chameleon or something. If I look at it out of the corner of my eye, it looks like a cartoon weasel or ferret, but with a face like a fox.

Really cute. So I duck into a bush and jump in front of it as it goes by.

"Sploot!" it screams, as I grab hold of its furry tail. "Sploot!" it shrieks again, trying to get away.

"Okay, okay! I won't hurt you. I just want to meet you!" I tell him, petting his soft fur. He immediately calms down and starts to lean in to my pets.

"Now, don't run away!" I say as I pet his long body and let go of his tail. He stretches out like a cat.

"Sploooot." He purrs, winds around my legs, and rubs against me.

"I think you like me." I keep petting his silky, soft fur as it changes colour from brown to tan to pink. "I hope everyone here is as friendly as you, Sploot." He sticks out his long tongue like he smells me with it.

Suddenly, Sploot takes off into the bush. Then I hear noises from up the road, getting louder. Maybe it's my friends! I can't wait to show them Sploot.

It is Matt and Celeste. But they're marching out in front, like prisoners. A group of hostile–looking aliens march behind them, holding spears.

"Hawk!" Celeste shouts when she sees me. She rushes over, followed by Matt.

"Looks like you found trouble," I whisper.

"Smells like you found a skunk!" Celeste says, holding her nose and stepping back.

The armed guard walks straight over to us, his red face twisted and angry. It looks like he's wearing a Halloween mask. A disgusting, drooling monster mask with bloodshot eyes, no nose, and all teeth. Ugh! He bows low. "Me Omega-Grog of Furilani," he bellows like we can't hear. He points to his chest, then at us, indicating we should say our names.

We all tremble and look down, away from his face.

"Me Hawk . . . I mean, I'm Hawk, and this is Matt and Celeste," I say. "We come from planet Earth."

"Why you come from planet Earth to Furilani?" he grunts his words from his nose. "Flek! What you want?" I translate for Celeste, leaving out the words I'm pretty sure she doesn't want to hear.

As we talk, Sploot creeps out from behind me, and Omega-Grog spots him, points with a hairy finger, and starts yelling.

"Get sploot! Flek! Get sploot!" He rushes toward the little creature as Sploot runs through my legs and into the long purple grass.

"Flek!" Omega roars as two of his henchmen go into the bush after him.

"Wait! He didn't do anything," I cry, watching the long grass part. The chase is on. The purple grass sways this way and that, as Sploot outsmarts them. The two brutes huff and puff and snort as they look around for the little sploot that got away.

"Flek!" bawls Omega again as his henchmen hang their heads and shuffle back toward us. Omega lashes out at them with his wide hairy foot, and they scurry behind him.

That's when I notice that Omega isn't wearing any clothes. He's covered in hair like Bigfoot or a Yeti. Ewwww!

"Why you take sploot?" he growls, eyeing us suspiciously.

"Um . . . we didn't *take* him anywhere. He followed me. I think he's just curious," I tell him.

"What's a 'sploot'?" Matt asks. He and Celeste look at each other and shrug.

"It's a cool pet," I tell them. "It's all furry and changes colour and . . ." I shut up when Omega raises his spear and shouts.

"Silence, thief! We will take you to our leader!" He nods his head up the road and nudges us with his spear.

"Did you hear that, Hawk? They're taking *us* to *their* leader!" Matt chuckles, then jumps as a guard pokes him with the pointy end of his spear. "Hey! Stop that! I'm going!"

I look back at the long purple grass for Sploot, but there's no sign of him. He must have turned purple.

CHAPTER 6

LIFE IN TECHNICOLOR

We march ahead of our captors and check out the cool scenery. I can't decide if it's more of a desert or a rainforest. It's a magical rainbow forest! Beyond the multi-coloured bushes, flowers float and bounce on their stems like the hairdryer and ping-pong ball science experiment our classmate, Sophie, did. Gravity holds the ball in place, even when she turned the hairdryer sideways! Super cool! Rows and rows of white sand dunes, separated by crystal clear pools of pink water. All the stones and pebbles shine like glass and reflect thc never-ending beaches of white sand. I shake my head to break the hypnotic illusion and . . . Wait! Pink water! Okaaaay.

In the distance, there is a huge volcano with hot pink rivers of lava that run down the mountainside. Or maybe it's a geyser. My grandpa took me to Yellowstone National Park, where they have more than half of the world's geysers. My favourite was 'Old Faithful'. It's called that because it erupts every two hours without fail. I couldn't believe it when I saw it for the first time. Hot water and steam shot up almost 200 feet in the air. I hope I get to see this one erupt!

I look away because the technicolor supernova is too much for my eyes. I wish I had the cool alien shades that Celeste gave me when we escaped from

the caves of Labyrinthia. We were down in the dark for so long that we had to block our eyes from the sun when we finally emerged. I jump as I feel the tip of Omega-Grog's spear poke my butt and realize that I've stopped. As we come up and over a small hill, there's a village in the distance that looks like a bustling alien marketplace. As we get closer, I see many different-looking aliens. Thankfully, they don't all look like Omega-Grog. Sorry, but he is one ugly dude!

We make a bit of an entrance as we are marched in like prisoners—*human* prisoners. Everyone stops and stares at us, and we gape back at them. It looks like a scene from the Alpha Cantina on *Star Trekkers*, our favourite TV show. The market has booths selling all kinds of weird goods. A starfish-faced alien puts down the bottle it was looking at, and a ten-armed green guy puts down ten items as half his face drops down to his chest. On the other side of the square, a non-humanoid space baby whines as its green-skinned mom covers the baby's head with her webbed arm. Matt and I look at each other as we stroll through town with all eyes on us. And I mean many, many eyes. This must be a spaceport for aliens to go shopping. I feel a twinge of hunger when I get a whiff of something delicious cooking on an outdoor grill. As we get closer, I see that it's a giant alien insect cooking over a fire with baskets of smaller bugs on the grill. I think of ANT-05 from Bilaluna with BBQ'd insect on a bun. He would not approve of this. I wouldn't eat it either; not even with my favourite drink, cola and milk, to wash it down.

Matt gasps. "Oh no! Not worms again!"

"At least they'll be grilled . . . not live worms, like last time!" I chuckle.

Celeste looks horrified because she really likes insects and wants to be a. . . . an ety-ologist or insec-tologist . . . Oh, whatever! A bug scientist, like Charles Darwin.

Omega growls behind us, and we walk. There are large transparent tubes halfway underground, and aliens pass through them very quickly. It's like an alien subway system. My eyes follow the tube stretch out of the spaceport village; it grows into a network of clear tubes leading to the sand dunes, out to the giant geyser, and beyond. Wow! Sometimes it spirals above ground, and you can see the riders passing through. What a way to travel—rapid transit, in a tube. It's like the Flume ride at Canada's Wonderland! I don't know where we're going, but I hope it's by the tube!

In front of us, many aliens line up at one of the stalls in the market. There are stacks of small cages, and every-one points and shouts. All the air is suddenly sucked out of me like a gut punch when I see the cages are full of sploots! The little creatures are dull and brown as they pace around in circles and look really scared.

"Hey! Why are the sploots in cages?" I motion toward a stand where a vendor sells the little animals. Matt and Celeste stop and look over curiously at the sploots.

"Sploot make nice cape. Everyone in galaxy want wear Furilani sploots," Omega says proudly.

"What?!" I say, turning to him. "Aliens wear other aliens?" I am appalled because I see something I hav-en't noticed before. Some of the aliens *are* wearing sploots! A long skinny guy has a light brown sploot tied around his middle like a belt. At the same time, a female being has a dark brown sploot around her thick neck like a scarf. I feel dizzy, like I might faint. I notice more and more sploots hanging on large aliens like earrings, headbands, and hats. What is going on here? The sploots' eyes are open, watching me, and sometimes they bite their own tails to form loops. At least they're alive! Not like on Earth, where minks, raccoons, and other animals are used for their fur to make coats for rich people. But it must be terrible to live as somebody's fashion accessory.

As we walk, I look back at the sad scene and wonder about the sploot I met. I'm glad he escaped, but maybe he needs help. Maybe his whole family will be sold at the market! I put it out of my mind for now because we are in front of a house that is halfway underground, like the tube. Omega bangs on a big gong with a mallet right next to me. I almost jump out of my skin. I block my ears and scowl at him. I'm not in a good mood right now. We hear noises from inside, then the door swings upward, almost sending me flying. A short grey alien with big eyes and a few hairs on his bald head stares at us.

He and Omega-Grog have a few words while Matt, Celeste, and I look around at the igloo-shaped houses that are mostly underground. I wonder if they do that to keep cool or to conceal them. From a drone or satellite's view, it would look like rolling hills. A big fountain in the middle of the alien village sprays pink water, like a smaller version of a geyser.

"Enter humans!" the doorman says, stepping aside.

We go inside, then Omega and his henchmen depart with a bow.

CHAPTER 7

LIFESTYLES OF THE RICH AND ALIEN

We enter the tiny house and find it's enormous inside. We follow the doorman down the ramp into a large chamber the size of a football field. It's like the Fortress of Silence on *Star Trekkers*, with massive white pillars from ceiling to floor. It's an underground mansion, and like most underground places, it's nice and cool down here. Suddenly, I get the creepy sensation that I'm being watched. I look at the tinted glass wall next to me, and I see movement behind it. I nudge Matt and nod toward the wall when something jumps and moves off. I think it was Omega-Grog. I'll never forget that face. Matt and I give each other a look—yeah, we're being watched. We try to catch Celeste's attention, but she just rubs her worry stone and avoids eye contact.

The doorman leads us to a long table covered with clear containers of what looks like weapons—grenades, bullets, batons. But the alien guy picks up the box of bullets and offers it to us.

"Protein log after your long journey?" He looks at us with crossed eyes that are different sizes and far apart.

I'm not sure where to look. But I hold up my hand and say: "Uh, thanks, but no thanks. I'm not hungry."

Matt and Celeste shake their heads and back away

from the container. The alien picks up a long hose and says, "Health water, perhaps?"

I step forward. "Oh yes, please. That sounds, um, healthy. I'll try some."

The alien butler turns the valve and sprays me from head to toe in pink health water. I am too shocked to do anything to get away from the spray. Matt and Celeste's eyes go wide, and they giggle. Thankfully the alien turns off the sprayer, and I drip on the floor like a wet rat. I realize how funny I must look, and I laugh too. It tastes delicious, and I feel refreshed.

Suddenly, a deep voice interrupts our laughter. "Unlike you, we instantly absorb health water through our outer membrane." To demonstrate, he picks up the hose and sprays his chest with healthy liquid pinkness, which disappears instantly. "Ahh, that's better." The saggy skin on his face quivers like Jell-O when he speaks. "Welcome to planet Furilani. Where all are welcome, as long as they come to trade goods. My name is V'alvlax, and our planet is home to alien beings from all over the galaxy—Mo'ots, Luxrns, and Be'rons, to name a few. Our embedded translator allows us to communicate with all intelligent beings. I came from planet Vo'lox to create this spaceport on Furilani. Every seller in the galaxy trades at our markets because of our reflecting stones and sploots. Now tell me, why are *you* here?" He's a tall, menacing alien with six eyes that he narrows at us. I notice he wears a belt around his middle, and at least ten sploots hold onto it with their teeth, swinging about as he moves.

"We came to your planet through a wormhole radio, sir," I say, shaking pink water out of my ears. "We thought your planet needed our help."

"Ha! Why would we need your help?" he leans close to our faces. "Are you not spies from planet Splooter?"

"What? No! Do we look like spies?" I cough.

"Actually, you do. Most spies wear ridiculous disguises like you have now." V'alvlax sneers at us, then reaches out toward Matt's face and tries to pull on his chin.

"Hey, don't do that." Matt steps back and puts his hands out in front of him. "This is my real face."

"Did you think you could fool us with your stubby appendages and nonporous cells?" He paces around the room as sploots fan out around him like a furry skirt.

Celeste and I look at each other, our eyes wide as Matt looks down at his short arms. "Okay, *we* are children from planet Earth . . . we are not in disguise; this is how Earthling children look. So don't insult my friends." My face gets hot and turns from healthy pink to red.

V'alvlax turns to us. "You want to steal our fashions and splooty-styles?"

"No way! We just want to help." I yelp as Omega-Grog runs in with his guards and grabs us. "Why are you wearing these animals anyway? How would you like to be some giant's scarf for the rest of your life?" I try to pull away from Omega's vice-like grip.

V'alvlax interrupts. "Insolent Earthlings! Take them away! Throw them in the tube and send them to the Exile Mountains. That's what we do with spies."

The sploots on his belt look sad and reach out to us with their long furry tails. At least we know who needs our help . . . *and yay! We're going on a tube ride!*

CHAPTER 8

EXILE MOUNTAINS

The tube is a wild ride. Now I know what a dust bunny feels like when it gets sucked into the vacuum cleaner! After he forced us into a clear capsule, Omega-Grog programs the tube for our one-way trip. He pushes a few buttons and his face breaks into an ugly grin. Our capsule slides in the pneumatic tube toward the mountains. I feel the hair on my neck prickle as we pick up speed and the g-forces get stronger. A sudden spin and we are all upside down but held in place by gravity. Our bodies shake from the twists and loops at five hundred miles per hour. Sometimes we see daylight as our capsule shoots above ground and back underground again. We all scream like we're on a roller coaster. But this is different—no sharp turns, no sudden impacts, and a soft, quick stop. We have reached our destination in ten seconds flat. When the top of the tube pops open, Matt, Celeste, and I fall over each other to get out of the pod on wobbly legs. We look like a couple of sardines trying to escape from a can.

"Where are we? There's no one around," says Matt.

"Maybe the tube let us out at the wrong stop," I guess.

"Or they leave us out here in the mountains to die," says Celeste as she reaches into her pocket for her stone.

"Watch out!" Celeste pushes me out of the way as the top of the tube closes shut, and the capsule disappears underground.

"Oof. Thanks." I feel dizzy, especially when I see where we are. We're high on top of a pink mountain surrounded by steep slopes on all sides. Everything is crazy colourful up here. Like neon colors. It hurts my eyes to look around.

"Look, you guys." Celeste points to one of the peaks that rumbles and shakes. Suddenly pink jets of water and mist shoot up into the sky. We notice steam and vapours rising from many hilltops, like an orchard of active geysers. Little pools of bubbling water steam and pop all around us. Some of them rumble and gurgle, threatening to erupt at any minute.

"We'd better get out of here. The water's boiling, and the vapours could be toxic." I grab Celeste's hand even though I know she doesn't like physical contact. Celeste tucks a strand of long hair behind her ear and hangs on as we head downhill. We avoid the steaming water, which is definitely not healthy water this time.

Matt trips, drops, and rolls headlong down the hill. Celeste and I look at each other and smile as we drop to the ground and roll as fast as possible to catch up with Matt. We end up at the bottom of the mountain in a tangle of arms and legs and laugh until tears run down our faces and we are covered in pink dust.

"That was fun," Matt says, still panting. "Oh, pink looks good on you, Hawk." He cracks up.

"Over here, guys." I stumble to my feet and make my way over to a little spring of warm water. "Let's get washed up and go rescue some sploots," I say, splashing water on my hair and face.

"What?! Do you really want to try to take away their clothes? V'alvlax will do more than shoot us into the mountains for that," Matt says, wading into the bath-like water.

"Yeah. I feel sorry for the sploots, but what can we do?" Celeste sits on the bank and touches the water with a finger before she washes her hands in it.

"We have to teach them that little sploots have a life too. And they can't buy and sell someone's life," I say, just before I do a cannonball into the creek.

"Wait! Hawk! No!" Celeste screams as a tidal wave of water crashes over her from my cannonball.

"Oops, Sorry, Celeste. I didn't mean to get you all wet." I try to hide my snicker. Then I notice Celeste's bottom lip quivering like she's going to cry. I wade over to her, feeling bad. "You'll be dry in no time . . ." I start to reach out to her when she leaps up and pushes me underwater.

"Take that, you dweeb." Celeste starts an epic splashing war that ends with all three of us soaked to the skin, but nice and clean. We sit in the rainbow grass to figure out a plan and dry in the warmth that emanates from the hillside.

"How do we convince them not to wear animals as the latest fashion?" Matt asks, looking up at the saucer-shaped clouds that hang over the distant mountains. Strangely, they look like UFOs.

"Maybe we can start a rebellion and convince the sploots to bite these hipsters and fashionistas right on the . . ." Celeste mutters. I think Celeste has been working on her assertiveness lately.

"I know!" Matt punches his palm. "We go back to the market and act sick around the sploots. Real sick. Then we say that sploots cause allergies." He looks around for approval.

Celeste cuts in, "Or we could go back and release all the sploots from the cages and bring them back here to the mountain. They'd love it up here. It's so peaceful."

"But like, those are just short-term solutions. They would figure out a sploot anti-allergy medicine or they would come up to the mountains and trap the sploots again." I pull at my tangled pinkish-blond hair. "It's hopeless," I say sadly. That's when I notice some large, hairy aliens heading our way with wooden swords, and I think they're licking their lips.

CHAPTER 9

BIGFOOT EXISTS

"**R**un!" Matt screams when he spots the hunting party.

"Don't bother, Matt. Have you seen the size of their feet? It's a whole clan of Bigfoots...err...Bigfeet. We could never outrun them. But maybe we can outsmart them instead. Follow my lead," I say under my breath. I raise my hands and nod at Matt and Celeste to do the same.

"Hello, Omega-Grog," I say, smiling a friendly greeting. The leader stops in his tracks and looks at me suspiciously.

"Omega-Grog my cousin, on mother's side. Me Omega-Slog," he says, looking around at his group, surprised by my greeting. "How you know cousin-Grog?"

"Yes . . . well . . . um . . . we're friends of his . . . from out of town. He gave us a tour of . . . of the market." I try to look sincere.

"We hungry, and you look like omega-food." He starts to drool a little and narrows his beady black eyes at us.

"No way, dude! We are definitely *not* food." I look over at Matt and Celeste, who shake their heads.

"You smell like omega-food too." He leans towards us and snuffles his large hairy nose, and the others in his group do the same.

I shake in my shoes because I don't want to be a Yeti-snack. Omega-Slog and his gang drool and get restless. That's when I notice that they all have razor-sharp teeth, like fangs. I rip one of my shoes off and throw it at them. "Here, eat this!" I yell. "Matt, Celeste! Let's get out of here! Run!"

Slog and his gang are surprised by the shoe, dive for it, and fight over it. Matt, Celeste, and I take advantage of the distraction and sprint down the mountainside as quickly as our stubby legs can carry us. I look back at the gang of Bigfoots and see one of them with his teeth clamped down on my shoe, shaking it like a dog. The slobber flies all over the place. *Sheesh. That is not a pretty sight.*

We dart from hill to hill to lose them, then flop down like fish out of water—gasping.

"I–think–we–lost–them." I pant. "But–now we're lost." I look down at my one shoe, and know I won't make it much further.

At that moment, I hear a soft chitter in my ear. When I turn my head, Sploot is there. "Hey, look, you guys! It's Sploot! The one that got away. Hi little guy." I reach toward him with my hand, and he backs up like he's afraid. "I won't hurt you, Sploot. I'm so glad to see you. Come say hello to Matt and Celeste." I reach out again, and this time he lowers his head to let me pet him, and inches closer to us. Matt and Celeste put out their hands to let Sploot smell them, and he lets them pet him too. Sploot rumbles and rubs against our legs.

"Listen, he purrs like a cat. I think he likes us," I say, just as Sploot turns a beautiful fuchsia colour.

"See! What did I tell you? He's like a chameleon or something," I cry.

"Wow, he's so pretty!" Celeste says, stroking Sploot instead of her stone.

"Maybe he's a she," Matt says, as he stares at the beautiful pink creature that bows its head in front of us. "My mom told me to say 'they' if I'm not sure if they're a girl or a boy."

Sploot shyly climbs onto my shoulder and rubs their head against mine. I look at Matt and Celeste with wide eyes, afraid to move.

"They sure do like you, Hawk," says Celeste, reaching over to pet Sploot, who changes from pink to multi-colours under her fingers. "Sploots are awesome!"

I stand up, and Sploot stays there, perched on my shoulder. But suddenly, Sploot jumps down and disappears into the trees. I look around for them as we are ambushed by Omega-Slog and his Bigfeet gang. Slog grabs Celeste, and the other two jump Matt and me. They tie us up with vines. I try to struggle free, but it's no use. The vines just get tighter.

Omega-Slog clears his throat. "Cousin Omega-Bog no like you tricky trick. We hungry and you smelling tasty!" He leans toward me and snuffles his nose in my hair. Sheesh, he looks like a hairier version of Grog . . . and doesn't smell nice either.

"Me thinks you three will taste better cooked. We put you in boiling unhealthy water for three to five minute." He laughs when he sees our horrified expressions. "No worry. Cousin-Bog chef of village." He looks over at the other Bigfoot standing nearby, and he pounds his chest.

"Bog, you help carry food to cooking pit."

"Wait," I say, trying to stall them. "I thought you said he was Bog?" I point at the other Bigfoot on the other side.

"That other cousin-Bog." Slog moves toward me, and I stiffen my body and throw my head back so that he can't pick me up. I look up into the blue tree above me and notice Sploot high up on a branch. I breathe a sigh of relief; at least Sploot is safe. Then I notice Sploot is pointing at something, and I see many turquoise-coloured sploots perched on the branches—lots of them—silently watching everything that's going on. They are all camouflaged.

Omega-Slog chuckles and says, "No bother to fight. You like bug in basket." Then he drools all over me. Blech. When Slog turns away to tighten the vines on Matt and Celeste, I struggle like mad to free myself. I look up into the branches to see what the clever sploots are doing. I can't see them anywhere. Then I notice some movement on the tree trunk. The sploots blend in with the tree and are almost invisible. If you didn't know better, like the Bigfeet, you wouldn't see them at all. When the two Bogs pick up Celeste and walk away with her, the camo-sploots creep down the tree trunk and cover Matt and me. It works like a cloak of invisibility! When Slog turns around his smile disappears, and he screams "Flek! Where you go?! Bog, wait. Where food go?" He runs off on his hairy feet after them. Matt and I waste no time getting untangled from the vines with the sploots' help. They chew through the vines like candy.

"Thanks team! C'mon Matt, we have to rescue Celeste." We all run in the direction they took Celeste. But Sploot chitters in my ear to stop and wait. "Matt, hold up. Sploot has a plan."

Sploot makes a kuk-kuk-kuk sound and points to a group of sploots, and they take off into the bushes. We watch and listen. We hear Slog's voice in the distance.

"There Bog. Our food go there!" We see the bushes sway this way and that way as the sploots make their way to a narrow path off to the left. At the end of the path, we see nothing but dead air. It must be a cliff.

Slog shouts again. "Put food down—it tied up. Heh-heh. Me want play 'hunter find prey' with other food. That fun." From our hiding spot in the bushes, we can hear him snickering, and it gives me chills.

All three Bigfeet charge down the path away from us and towards their suspected prey in the long purple grass. We turn around to find Celeste, who has freed herself with some help from the sploots. Then we run to a bush where we can watch all the action. Sploot points out two sploots to us. They crouch on either side of the path and turn themselves purple to match the long grass. Then, seconds before the Bigfeet pass, they join their mauve tails and twist them together across the path. We cheer when we hear the wails of the Bigfeet as they trip over sploot tails and tumble down the cliff and out of sight.

Sploot gives me a high-five as their coat turns from purple into a rainbow of colours. Matt and Celeste jump up and down and cheer for the clever sploots.

CHAPTER 10

IT'S A SPLOOT'S LIFE

"Hey, Hawk, Sploot is pointing in that direction," Matt says. "Let's walk that way. Maybe it's a shortcut to the village."

"You're right, Matt," says Celeste. "Look, there's a route through the pink forest."

"Yeah. Sploots are really smart." I walk with Sploot, who leads the way. We continue down the mountain along a path that is thick with pink and red bushes. I step carefully, so I don't disturb Sploot, who watches us and points the best way down. Sploot sniffs the air, jumps off my shoulder, and scurries toward the base of a hill and starts digging.

"Sploot! What is it?" I call out, running to the hillside. Sploot doesn't turn around and digs until an opening appears in the pink grass. We help Sploot clear the pathway and see stairs leading into the mountain.

Matt peeks in. "Cool! It's a secret passageway."

I look down at the little creature covered in pink dirt and dust. "Did you smell this?" I ask Sploot, who nods and twirls around my legs. They push me toward the stairs which leads to darkness. "Let's go, guys. Sploot's a genius."

"Maybe we should stay out here? I'm trying to forget the last time we went 'caving'," Celeste says, rubbing her worry stone.

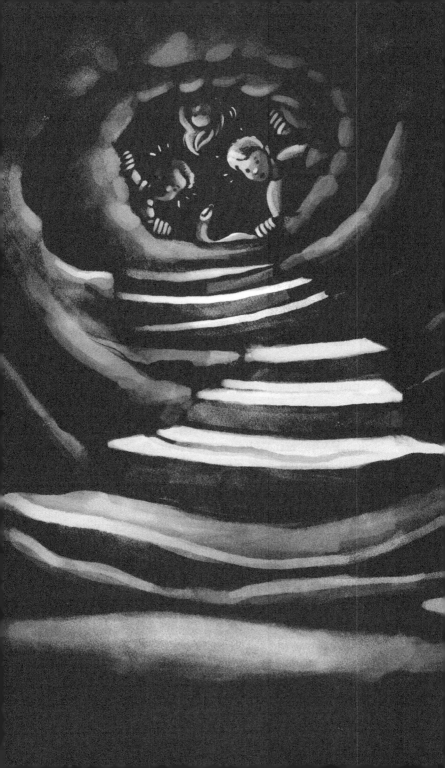

"I trust Sploot, Celeste. They want to show us something. But we'll come back up here if it gets too scary." I reach out my fist to show her my space club ring, and she touches it with her ring. We look at Matt, who joins our circle of rings.

"Yippee Ki-Yay! Let's do it," shouts Matt, and we start down the stairs where Sploot patiently waits for us.

"What's that thing?" asks Celeste, pointing ahead of us.

"It looks like a lava tube," I say. "A tunnel made by lava that flowed down from a volcano.""But it's so smooth." Matt's eyes almost pop out.

"It looks like the waterslide at Splash Mountain."

"I bet the sploots use it to get down the mountain fast," I guess. "It's like a sploot-tube."

Before I know it, Sploot jumps off my shoulder and slides down the long tube into the darkness. Before vanishing, the little creature looks back and beckons us with a paw.

Celeste hesitates, then jumps into the tube and disappears into the darkness.

I grab Matt's hand and we both close our eyes and jump in after her, yelling, "Yippee Ki-Yay!"

It gets darker and darker as we speed down the lava tube. Luckily, the hillside walls have cracks that let in dusty beams of pink light overhead. We follow Sploot, down, down, down the slide, then the grade flattens as we cross a long narrow bridge where the walls and ceiling of the lava tube open up. This journey down the sploot tube was even faster than the tube Omega

Grog threw us in, but now we slow down. There is pink water on either side of the bridge, and it must be hot springs because it is steaming down here. Now and then we hear steam hissing from the walls.

"Whew! I'm about to melt, Hawk. I can't take much more of this heat." Matt wipes the back of his hand across his sweaty brow.

"Yeah, my brain is about to explode like the popcorn in your science experiment," Celeste says, leaning over with her hands on her knees.

We stop at the far side of the bridge, and Sploot, who is still ahead a little, sits up like a prairie dog and looks around the wide opening at the base of the mountain. Something shifts in the dark and many little eyes sparkle and look at us. The walls and ledges are covered in sploots. Since they are chameleons, they blend into the background; it's their defence mechanism.

We are all silent because we don't want to scare them, but we are in awe.

"So, this is where you hide," I say, looking around. "Good plan. The fashion police will never find you here. But it's so hot down here."

Sploot chitters, and a group of them emerge from the shadows. They creep toward me, and I stick out my hand to let them smell me. Before I know it, they are all over me. I panic for a second as I'm buried in creatures. I look around and see Matt and Celeste laugh and pet excited sploots. I can't believe it; it's like a sploot party. They are so happy to see us; they lick our faces and tickle us. We are still chuckling when I notice the sploots farthest from us are different colours. Their fur is brown and dull. But the ones we pet shimmer into the most beautiful colours I've ever seen.

Sploot chitters again, and the others calm down and sit on the ground, looking at us expectantly. Matt, Celeste, and I pull ourselves together, and Sploot jumps back on my shoulder. They lick my face and nods their silky head up and down.

"We want to help all of you," I say. "So you don't have to hide inside a hot mountain or be locked in a cage until someone chooses you for their hat." I look at how brilliant Sploot looks as I scratch the fur behind their ears. "We'll show those posers a better fashion sensation."

"What are you talking about?" puzzled Celeste.

"Listen, everyone." I tap my temple. "Did you notice that the sploots used as scarves and belts were a dull colour? White, brown, and grey?"

"Yeah, it's true. I didn't notice any brightly coloured sploots anywhere in the market or at V'alvlax's place." Matt says.

"But what does that have to do with anything?" Celeste asks.

"We could show them that loving these little creatures and treating them right makes them happy. And making them happy turns their fur to beautiful colours."

"But that'll make them want to wear them even more," Celeste cries.

"No. Because if they abuse sploots, or force them to be hats and scarves, or lock them in cages, they go back to dull colours," I say while petting Sploot.

"Hmmm. It might work. Now, if we could get out of this mountain," Celeste says, flipping her smooth stone between her fingers to help her concentrate.

"Right! Everyone will want a sploot to love. Like a teeny-tiny version of Wolfie," Matt says. "They wouldn't wear their pets . . . would they?"

"No, of course not," I say. "That's the beauty of it. They would *want* their sploots to be the most beautiful colours possible. So they would keep them very happy."

"Feed them the best food," Matt says.

"Groom and brush their fur," Celeste adds.

"Pet them and carry them around everywhere." I slap my knee. "Ha ha! I can see V'alvlax now, as his rainbow sploot rides around on his shoulder." I get up and walk like a model down an imaginary catwalk with Sploot on my shoulder. Celeste covers her mouth and giggles. Some of the sploots follow me and walk upright on their hind legs. They stop when I stop and walk when I walk, copying me. When I look back, they look back. Matt throws his head back, and belly laughs until a rosy little sploot leaps onto his shoulder, startling him. He and the sploot look at each other, then Matt stands up and follows me. He swings his hips and takes small steps like a fashion model. We stop and look at Celeste over our shoulders with a duckface, and the sploots do the same.

"Okay, okay, you guys!" Celeste says, doubling over with laughter. "I can't take anymore. I get it; they're good at this."

CHAPTER 11

THE FASHION POLICE

Sploot shows us another underground shortcut that leads to the market. They use it like an underground railroad to help other sploots escape from the market.

"My dad told me all about the Underground Railroad from Earth's history," Matt says as we pick our way downhill. Matt's dad is African American. "It wasn't underground or even a train. It was a bunch of people, of all races, who helped runaway slaves go from one hideout to another until they got to a place where slavery was illegal, and they could be free."

"Cool, freedom fighters! Hey, let's be freedom fighters for the sploots," Celeste says, and gives Matt a high-five. The sploots turn and give each other a high-paw.

"Gosh, these sploots are real smart," I say, looking at *my* sploot, who lifts a paw to me. *When did I start saying 'my sploot'?*

"Look! Up ahead, it's brighter, and I can see an opening in the wall. C'mon!" Matt says, starting to run. I notice the ground leveling out as we make our way toward the narrow crack which lets us out of the hillside. A rock juts out above the crack, casting a shadow that hides the opening during the day.

"Let's make sure the coast is clear before we go outside," I tell them. Sploot makes a kuk-kuk-kuk sound, and all the other sploots line up like little soldiers. I marvel at how polite they are as I peek through the crack in the wall and look left and right. "Okay, let's go!"

We squeeze through the opening and see that we are surrounded by pink pools that have run off the mountain. Sploot jumps out in front to lead us from sandbar to sandbar to avoid getting wet again as we head back to the market. Our leader looks back often to make sure the other sploots keep up and stay in line, but it isn't long before we have fun, skipping and kicking the warm water as we run. Suddenly the marketplace shimmers in the distance like an oasis in the desert. We all slow to a stop.

"There it is!" shouts Matt, pointing, and we all look at him in shock. Even the sploots.

I put my finger to my lips. "Shhhhhh!" All the sploots look at Matt with a paw to their little mouths, and they all turn a dull gray. We creep forward from one rainbow bush to another, closer and closer to the bustling marketplace. We could blend into the crowd, if only we could disguise ourselves. I look around for something, anything, to cover our identity. I turn to ask Celeste what to do, but she's covered from head to toe in brown sploots. Except for her eyes, which blink at me from between two sploots' tails wrapped around her face. Behind her, Matt looks like a surprised Chewbacca from Star Wars. "Whoa!" I start to laugh, but I stop when all the rest of the sploots jump on me and slither around my body until the three of us are standing there like we are on our way to a Wookiee convention.

We creep along a small road that leads to the marketplace. I'm waiting for someone to notice we are fugitive Earthlings dressed like sploot mummies, but nobody even looks at us twice as they shop, haggle, and trade. The aliens look strange, maybe stranger than we do—tall aliens with no faces, round aliens with only hands for limbs, and long aliens with sharp teeth. Most have dull brown or grey sploots around their necks or waists. Oh brother, it's like Halloween, only it's for real.

The road is dotted with little pods offering services. Screens in front of each pod show aliens eating, sleeping in hammocks, and working out. I scan all the images that show a restaurant, motel, and gym, I guess . . . or maybe it's lightsaber training? One store has a picture of an omega Bigfoot with his mouth wide open, showing razor-sharp teeth. *Sheesh, I hope it's a dentist's office.* We try to blend in and look like we're just casual shoppers, but it's hard to see with sploots on your face. Celeste loses her balance, and teeters from one side of the road to the other as aliens jump to get out of her way. Matt and I catch up to her and take an elbow to help her walk, but we stumble too! We come upon large, yellow slugs with tennis ball eyes on the road in front of us, and we slip around in their slime trails. *Gross!*

"S'cuse us." I mumble as we side-step the slime to get to the sploot shop. Whew! I'm getting hot under all this fur. Speaking of fur, the fur is flying at the sploot stall. A purple and green alien are fighting over the last two sploots on the shelf.

"I want one for each of my heads." The giant, green two-headed alien vibrates and speaks in stereo with two whiny voices.

"I'll zap one of your heads, and then you won't need so many hats. I'm not leaving here without a sploot." The larger purple alien pushes the green alien out of the way and reaches for the cage. The sploots cling to each other and tremble at the back of the cage, as white as sploots can be.

"I was here first! Help! Furi-Police!" The green being screams from both heads in harmonizing voices.

Almost immediately, a round transparent bubble appears over our heads. It drops out of the sky and lands next to us. We slither aside so we aren't detected and watch two robots inside the bubble.

"Halt! You are under arrest for threatening bodily harm!" A robotic voice says through a speaker. Then a net slingshots out of a hole in the bubble and ensnares the purple alien as he struggles to get loose.

"Let me go!" He screams as the bubble shoots into the sky, hauling the net behind it.

"That was cool! But don't break any laws, you guys!" I whisper to the others. "The Furi-fashion police are watching."

"Oh no, look!" Matt points, and all our heads turn at the same time.

The green alien walks away with the cage, *and* the last two sploots!

CHAPTER 12

FANCY SPLOOTS

In a blinding flash of fur, Sploot leaps off my head and flies after the disappearing cage. The two sploots inside grab the bars and look back at us miserably before the alien covers them with a shade. Matt, Celeste, and I look at each other and, with a nod, we stagger and stumble to catch up to them. Suddenly, Sploot and his buddy disappear into the scenery. We freeze with our mouths agape before it occurs to us: chameleon camouflage! We watch the magic happen. One sploot squeals and the two green heads stare off in the direction of the noise. Then, hippity hop, one, two, three—the cage door opens, and the two sploots inside are replaced with two rocks. Imagine the green alien's surprise when he pulls back the drape and looks for his new hats. Matt and Celeste chuckle and high-five—point scored for Team Sploot! All four sploots race back to us, and Sploot and his partner in crime jump back on my head. The other two find available spots to ride on Matt and Celeste. We all teeter-totter back to the Sploot stall just as the seller closes up shop for the day.

"Um, excuse me. Do you have any more sploots?" I stammer, afraid a net is going to grab me from above.

"No! I'm all sold out." He doesn't even look at us. "Don't bother me, or I'll call the Furi-Police," he snaps.

"No, that's okay. I'll come back tomorrow." I hold up my hands as I back away.

"Don't bother. We have to wait to get more from the farm. The sploots aren't reproducing," he says, walking away with his sploot sign.

"What does that mean?" I call after him.

"Don't you *know* anything? It means they have no babies for us to sell."

We all look at each other with our mouths open. *Whaaaa...*

"Wait!" Matt yells after the quickly departing alien, "Where is this farm?"

"I don't know. No one knows. It's a heavily guarded secret," he says as he jumps into the tube and gets sucked away. We trudge back the way we came.

"What do we do now?" Celeste cries as she rubs her worry stone and looks around at all the glum faces. The sploots have slid off us, and we sit down in a pink meadow near the base of the mountain. We watch the sploots chatter to each other.

"Can we bring them back to Planet Splooter?" asks Celeste. "We can make a stopover on our way back to Earth."

"I wish it were that easy, Celeste. But they'd probably just go back there and trap them again. No, we have to teach them that sploots are not property, and they deserve love and respect."

Suddenly the sploots start to play with each other. We watch them chase each other and tumble down the hill while they change their fur colours. It's mesmerizing, like a rolling rainbow! We laugh our heads off as we watch the sploot show. Sploot-watching should be a competitive sport.

"Hey!" says Matt, petting the sploot beside him. "Let's have a sploot parade to show off all the amazing things sploots can do. I know what you're going to say, it's a silly idea, and— "

"No, Matt! That's brilliant!" I say, and I mean it. "Sploots are intelligent, curious, gifted creatures who shouldn't be treated like clothing." I raise my hand for a high-five, and all the sploots do the same.

"I love it! Let's show them that sploots matter," says Celeste. "We can teach them some tricks, then put up signs in the market about it and make floats, and oh, did I tell you that I know how to juggle?"

We all look at Celeste in surprise. She hasn't been this excited about anything since we met cyborg insects on Bilaluna. And *no*, we didn't know she could juggle . . . but she does have telekinetic powers!

We spend the rest of the day planning a parade. Who knew there could be so much to do to put a parade together? Some sploots go off in another direction after a huddle with their leader. I think they know where the mysterious farm is, and they're going on a sploot rescue mission. We need some supplies for the show, so when Sploot comes back and jumps on my shoulder, we head back into town. We are looking for cardboard or wood, paint, costumes, and maybe a cart. We sneak from pod to pod, looking for something useful. Behind the alien restaurant we find some big boxes and a wagon we 'borrow' to put everything in.

There's a convenience pod still open, and we decide it's worth the risk to go in and get some paint and brushes to create colourful signs and floats. We all walk into the store and look around in wonder. So much weird stuff, all inside transparent cupboards; you can see, but you can't touch the merchandise. Some of the cubbies hold alien sports gear, alien toys, and alien food. Which reminds me—we missed lunch today. Suddenly, a clear cupboard door pops open, and we see a large bag inside. We all look at one another, not sure what to do next. A voice says, "Please take your articles, and thank you for shopping at Space-Mart." I reach into the cubby and take the bag, and we hurry toward the exit. Can it be this easy? We are just about to exit the store when we hear the same voice say: "Insufficient Funds! Insufficient Funds! Stop! By order of the Furi-Police."

"Uh-oh! Who has money?" I check my pockets, but there's just a dime and two lint-covered Tic Tacs. The security alien runs over to grab us, and the other shoppers stop to watch. I hold out the Tic Tacs, and he pauses, and looks at the candies in my hand. He frowns and says, "your memory bank has insufficient funds."

"My what?" I exclaim.

"Your memory bank. This is a memory-store pod, and you trade memories for goods. Unfortunately, your . . ."

Just then, Matt pulls his crystal out of his pocket and holds it out to the guard. Everyone stops and stares at the pulsating, colourful crystal in his hand. The security guard's eyes go wide, as he touches the prism and fills himself with energy from it. Then he drops down to bow in front of us. All the onlookers gape, then bow down too.

The store manager approaches Matt and says, "Many pardons, Master!"

CHAPTER 13

MASTER MATT

First, my memories are not good enough, and now Matt's a Master? A Master what? The prism glows brighter. Okay, this may work for us. I give Matt a quick thumbs up, and he nods.

"We are honoured that you chose our Space-Mart, Master." The store manager bows low. "Only great Masters have the shoq-lot energy crystal." He points around the shop. "What else can we offer you? You just have to think about it, and we will fulfill all your needs." The guard stands in front of us, and he shifts his eyes to look at the prism warily, while the store manager beams.

In complete 'Matt style,' we are carried through the store and into a strange elevator that not only goes up and down but sideways. It zigzags and takes a short corkscrew route before it lets us out in a neon-coloured, multi-dimensional carnival playground. It's like we woke up in a spectacular shared dream. There's a Ferris wheel, rocket ship, balloon spinners, virtual games, and everything is covered in neon lights. I can't believe my eyes! Did Matt think all this up? Even our hosts are amazed.

We run over to the Ferris wheel and climb into the carriage for a ride to the top. We are so excited right now that we can't talk. The wheel starts to turn, and we slowly climb to the top and get an awesome view of the whole park. Then we descend on the other side. Matt and Celeste laugh, and Sploot hides inside my hoodie. At the bottom, we jump out and run to another ride. We want to try them all! But then we notice the food counters; carnival food is the best! There are corndog popsicles, deep-fried cookies, Furilani funnel cake, and all sorts of interesting foods on sticks. I always thought there should be more food on sticks, so I am excited by all the caramel alien apples, bagel lollipops, and octopus-tentacle kebabs. Okay, I'm not so thrilled about the tentacle kebabs, but everything else is crazy good.

We don't realize how hungry we are until Matt's brain brings up food, and amazing things to eat appear. I think my head is about to explode. What is going on here? I look over at Matt and Celeste, who stuff their faces with deep-fried noodles and veggie balls on a stick. I try to make sense of the situation. The security guard wanted to arrest us until he saw Matt's prism, and then he treated Matt like a king or a VIP. I mean, the prism gives Matt a superpower over these beings. Holy cow! We can get the Space-Mart to help us plan the sploot parade. This is awesome!

"Hey, Matt!" I elbow him to get his attention. "If you think about all the things we need for the parade, maybe the Space-Mart will do it for us." I raise my eyebrows and wink at him. Matt nods and takes another bite of his butter-battered, cotton-candy kebab, and his eyes widen as he realizes what I mean.

"Right! We'll have loads of help with the parade now." Matt smiles and gobbles up the rest of his kebab.

"This is great!" Then he frowns. "But what do you think the prism does?"

"I think it has energy. And energy is power. They must really value the energy the prism can store. But only Masters get to have prisms." I take a big slurp of my corndog popsicle. Mmm, so good.

"Well, I can read your mind." He stares down at the crystal, which glows even more. "Maybe all your thoughts are here now."

Sploot trembles in my hoodie, but eyes my corndog with curiosity. I offer them a piece of frozen cornmeal. Sploot likes it! But I don't think they like the aliens at the Space-Mart; they've been used and abused by this society, and don't trust them.

We go on a few more rides, but my stomach rumbles and gurgles; Matt and Celeste look a bit sick too. So we find a quiet corner and put our heads together. I pet Sploot's fur.

"This is going to be great. A sploot parade!" I start. "Celeste, all we have to do is think of what needs to be done, and the Space-Mart will do it for us."

"Thanks to Master-Matt." Celeste giggles. "Who knew?"

Matt laughs and puffs out his chest. "I like that name. It has a nice ring to it. Hey! You guys can call me Busta Masta-Matt."

"Ha! You a rappin-rat, Matt!" I start making beatbox sounds with my mouth, and Celeste joins in with a drumbeat on her leg. Matt saunters around and raps.

"I'm Masta-Matt–I'm telling you that.
"Don't go wearing no sploot hat.
"In a place called space–I'm the human race
"I'm here with my homies–no one else knows me"
Matt pauses for effect.
"I have prism-power–for a Furilani-hour
"Come join the parade–on a sploot crusade
"In the arcade with Masta Ratt-Matt
"Respect...in!
Accept...in!
Connect...in!
"It's the sploot-crusade in!"

Matt starts hip-hopping to the beat and chanting the chorus. *"Respect...in! Accept...in! Connect...in!"*

Woohoo! We're dancing and slide-stepping to the beat. Man, we have *got* to have this in the parade!

CHAPTER 14

EVERYONE LOVES A PARADE

Matt asks the Space-Mart to organize the sploot parade for us and we decide to have it the next afternoon. Matt uses his imagination to think of everything: costumes, music, floats, and of course, lots of sploot shows. He needs to give them a detailed picture because they have no idea what a parade is. At first, they are a little confused.

"Aha, your parade is like our traffic jams in the port!" the Space-Mart owner says.

"No, a parade is more like a celebration," Matt says patiently.

"Ahh, now I know. A parade is like our annual old-ness fete." The manager nods solemnly.

"Um, no. That sounds like a birthday party. A parade is a bunch of people walking along the street dressed in costumes and waving balloons," Matt explains.

"Ah, now I see. It's like our ceremony of the dead. Is there candy too?" he asks. Matt rolls his eyes and looks over at me for help.

"Let me think about the best parade I've ever seen and all the details I can remember, to help you under-stand." Matt holds out the crystal for the store man-ager to put his hand on and he tells me to think of the best parade I ever saw while he reads my mind.

I visualize the parade my grandpa took me to in Montreal. It was awesome. There were colourful costumes and floats with moving parts like dinosaurs, robot chickens, giant inflated Spiderman, and of course Tom the Turkey. I thought of all the marching bands, dancers, and acrobats we'd seen, creating the procession of excitement and delight.

"Now I understand," the manager says. "We will help you create the best parade Furilani has ever seen." He turns to Matt. "We will honor you and make you proud, Master. Just one more question: who will be the fat man in the red suit with the white hairy face?"

"Oops, never mind about that," I say, blushing. I turn and look at the others. "Okay! Listen up everyone. We have little time to do a lot of stuff. You all know your jobs, so let's get to work and make this the greatest show on Furilani." Then I see the army of Space-Mart workers nod and scurry about getting stuff done. They chitter and chat with each other as they create beautiful costumes and floats, design sets, and practise skits for the first-ever Furilani parade.

We return the next morning and see that the Space-Mart staff have worked all night. There's a special float for 'Masta-Matt' and his entourage (that's me and Celeste), and a special sploot float to show off the importance of our furry friends. They announce the event on their social media for maximum universal exposure. All the electronic billboards in Furilani advertise the parade as a not-to-be-missed intergalactic event! They send out holographic invitations to all the inhabitants' AI. The message said to be there and pay respect to the Master. There are videos every-where that display hip-hop aliens, acrobatic clowns, and jugglers. They've never seen anything like it. The whole spaceport is abuzz, and aliens arrive in droves from other planets to see the show. We are going metagalaxy-viral!

Bang! Bang! Bang!

It sounds like someone is trying to bang down the Space-Mart door. An alien clown opens it, and Omega-Grog and his friends stand there. He seems a little taken aback by the clown, but quickly composes himself. When he sees us, his eyes open wide, and he screams.

"Flek! How you get here?"

"Hi, Omega! We met your cousin, Slog. He said to say hi to you," I say cheerfully.

Omega sneers and tries to walk into the room, but the Space-Mart workers block him. "Omega-Slog an oaf. I see you outwit him and escape!" He tries to push towards us, his ugly face turns dark red, then purple, but the Space-Mart guards stop him.

"Hand over the fugitives! V'alvlax will hear about dis." The workers raise their weapons and one of them leans over and whispers something to Omega.

"Graar! I don't care about crystal. V'alvlax will shut you down." Omega rages and splutters as he is pushed out of the shop. "Then we will see who is Master." Omega's lips curl into an ugly smile. He cackles, then chokes.

Matt shakes his head. "Sheesh. What a grouch!" He turns back to prep his band of alien-rap backup

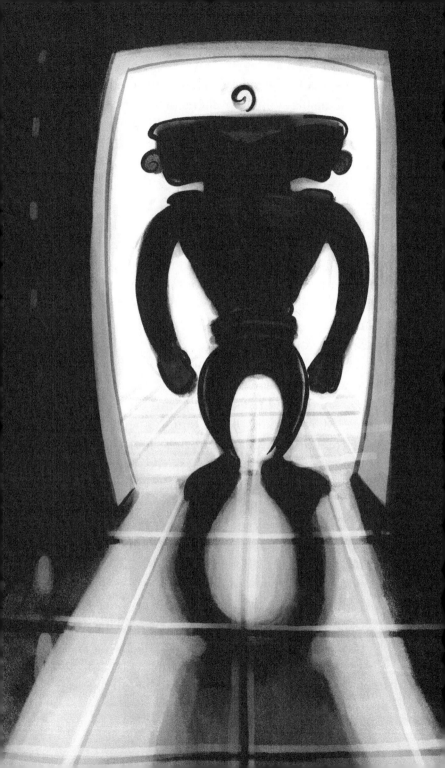

singers. He teaches them hip-hop dance moves, and Celeste and I are the audience. The little aliens look gangsta as they lean back with their arms crossed, and they lock, bop, and stare with attitude. Then Matt teaches them the cabbage patch—they make circular motions with their little fists and long, bony arms as they lean into it. We clap and tell them how fantastic they will be in the parade.

Celeste practices her juggling act and has decided to juggle sploots to highlight their fun nature. I sort out the floats and musicians. I've taught some of the sploots how to play basketball, and we'll have a float with a small court, with a basket at each end and a sploot-sized ball. Matt has thought up the perfect alien marching band, and the Space-Mart has all the right instruments and costumes. It's going to be great! Everything is almost ready, and not a moment too soon. We want V'alvlax to see the parade and appreciate the happy, colourful sploots. We hope Omega-Grog will get him here in time for the sploot show.

CHAPTER 15

SPLOOTS ON PARADE

It's show time and we all vibrate with excitement. The sploots enjoy their freedom in the carnival playground. After Matt *thinks* away the noisy carny rides, he changes the scene to include some edible plants and colourful trees with tree houses and zip-lines for the energetic sploots to play on. Of course, we keep the games and food—sploots love corndog dough. The sploots feel safe and comfortable in their peaceful new shire we called Splootsville.

I enter Splootsville and see Matt and Celeste play ring-toss with their cinnamon-bacon bagels before scarfing them down. I look up into the trees for Sploot. It's our game. We play an alien version of "Where's Waldo," and I have to find Sploot camouflaged among the trees, flowers, and bushes. It's not easy, but I finally spot them in a soft nest under some bushes, chattering with friends. I approach the nest on my hands and knees to surprise them when something leaps at me out of the blue.

"Aaaah! Ha ha ha! You got me again, Sploot!" I laugh and fall flat on my face while Sploot dances around on my back. "What are you doing back there? That tickles." I squirm and giggle as Sploot's little paws tickle me up and down my spine.

Celeste looks for us and interrupts our play. "C'mon you guys! Everything's ready! Let's go." She shouts and runs off.

Suddenly all the sploots run from the woods toward us. Sploot screams and dives for cover under my chin. I protect my little buddy, then we climb to our feet and follow the rest of the gang to the start of the parade route.

The Space-Mart employees run around doing sound checks, float inspections, and last-minute preparations for the big spectacle. I look out the window, amazed to see the crowds of aliens from all over the galaxy lined up in anticipation. We've advertised this as the event of the universe, and we have to deliver. No pressure! I start to sweat as the procession finally rolls out from behind the Space-Mart. I dart my eyes around as I look for V'alvlax or Grog, but I don't find them anywhere. Where are they? This parade has to impress V'alvlax enough for him to free our friends from sploot-slavery.

The first float is for the popular three-headed Lady Mayor, her Minister, and the Ambassador of Furilani. The mayor is in a big pink flatbed vehicle with her entourage; she waves and triple-smiles at the adoring crowd. Right behind her is a giant-sized colourful balloon shaped like a sploot. It floats and bounces above the audience, attached to ropes pulled by a self-driven ATV. All the young aliens are delighted as the sixty-foot sploot bobs and weaves over their heads. So far so good!

I realize it's almost time for the rappin' Masta-Matt show. I run out back and join Matt and Celeste on the coolest parade float ever. The stage is set with a big bandstand

and a cool alien DJ doing the beat-box sounds in his huge headphones and dark shades. It's already rolling, or should I say, hovering along—this float actually floats. The music is booming as Matt and his posse of alien gangstas be-bop and hip-hop on the stage. It's exciting as our floating stage pulls into the parade procession with the volume on max. Rhythmic beatbox, turntable scratches, chants, and synthesizer basslines get the alien audience pumped up and gaping at the show in awe. The crowd roars as we hover through the middle of town, and Masta-Matt starts rappin' about how sploots matter. Celeste and I do our hip-hop moves to get everyone breakdancing.

"I'm Masta-Matt–I'm telling you that.
"Don't go wearing no sploot hat.
"In a place called space–I'm the human race
"I'm here with my homies–no one else knows me

Matt pauses for effect, then repeats the last part as the crowd joins in and chants along with him. The sploots change colours and jump from one alien to another. They make the audience cheer as they give high-fives and low-fives to everyone on stage.

Matt raps his song, then he pulls out his prism and waves it around so the crowd can see it. They scream and applaud their excitement. Some aliens appear to be crying. It's Matt-Mania!

"I have prism-power–for a Furilani-hour
"Come join the parade–on a sploot crusade
"In the arcade with Masta Ratt-Matt."

The whole town swoons to the rhythm and the beat. Matt and his band keep them entertained while Celeste, Sploot, and I slip away and get ready for our own acts. Celeste gets her sploot juggling partners together and lines up behind the Space-Mart float that tosses snacks and colourful beads to the excited aliens who jostle to catch a prize.

Celeste marches forward and the sploots climb up the ladder on the float in front of her and leap through the air into her hands. She tosses one after another up into the air. They twist and turn into furry balls as they spin. The crowd cheers as the sploots cascade down in a rainbow of colours, each more beautiful than the last. The colourful sploots land on the railing of the float, then run around the outer edge and leap back to Celeste to be tossed into the air again. It's an amazing show of balance, timing, and skill.

After Celeste tosses them a few more times, they do a new trick. Celeste tosses one up in the air and it spins and changes colour, then she tosses two sploots up and they spin and change colour before they rain down. One up, two up; one up, two up. She gets a rhythm going and increases it to two up, two down. The audience enjoys this display of sploot creativity and skill. The remaining sploots sit on the railing and wait their turn to spin or run around the edge of the float and blow kisses to the crowd. Their fur changes colours as they zip around the float. Celeste has done a fantastic show of sploot love for the Furilani onlookers. I hope V'alvlax is in the crowd!

CHAPTER 16

DON'T HAVE A SPLOOT-ATTACK

It's my turn to wow the crowd. I hope our basketball game works as well as the rapping and the juggling! I sweat bullets again as the two sploot teams get in place on the basketball court float. A huge Jumbotron screen shows all the action and close-ups for maximum effect. The Space-Mart created tiny, sleeveless basketball jerseys or pop-tops for the players that show off their furry bellies. The jerseys are made of iridescent gold and silver colours that shimmer and sparkle like soap bubbles. I'm the ref, and Sploot, on my shoulder, is the mascot.

I toss a small basketball up between the two teams and they jump for it. The sploot gold team captain grabs the ball and dribbles it down the court. The sploot silver team sets up a defence to try and steal the ball, just like I showed them. The gold team passes the ball from one player to another until one of them is close enough to sink a basket. The crowd cheers as they start to understand the object of the game and get into it.

The sploots are like the Harlem Globetrotters! They play the game, but they do it with style. They show off their comedic timing and skills as they dribble and pass the ball back and forth on the court while performing acrobatic tricks. One silver team player is the

star of the game as they weave in and out of the other team's defence. The star sploot slam-dunks the ball after bouncing the ball off the backboard to alley-oop it to themself. Everyone shouts and cheers for one team or the other. The game gets a little serious when the score is all tied up and both teams try their best to score the winning point. The crowd goes wild as one player bounces the ball back and forth across the court and the other sploots do flips and somersaults to get into position.

Finally, before the buzzer goes off, one of the gold team sploots steals the ball and jumps up, bouncing off of everyone's head and shoots the ball toward the hoop. We're all holding our breath as the ball flies through the air and . . . swish! It drops through the basket with the sploot still hanging on to it.

The gold team wins the game! They are up on the giant screen as they cheer and high-five each other. Then the silver team does the same! They are just happy to play the game and show off!

Matt and Celeste come and join us on our float, which is the last one in the parade. There's hip-hop music playing, and we all dance and celebrate. We stop to let the aliens come aboard the float to meet the now famous sploots. Some of the teenage aliens rush over to where Masta-Matt is standing with his hip-hop bandmates and ask them to share their dance moves. A younger one runs over to the basketball court and ties to grab a sploot.

"Whoa there." I stand in front to block her. "I don't think they like to be picked up like that."

"Why not? That's what they're for," answers the little alien with five pink ponytails and purple skin.

"Here, try it like this." I take her limb and gently stoke the sploot, who starts to purr. "Be gentle with the sploot."

"Why are they called sploots?" she asks.

"That's the only word they can say when they want something. Also, what they do when they lie down on their bellies with their back legs stretched out behind them. It's called splooting." Sploot complies and stretches out their hind legs, turning a beautiful pink, purple, and orange colour.

"Ooh that's a coolio colour. I want a hat like that," she declares.

I stand up and grab the microphone. "Listen up everybody. My friends the sploots are just like you; they are inhabitants of this planet. They don't want to be worn as clothing or bought and sold like merchandise. They just want to be loved and respected." Sploot leaps onto my shoulder and rubs up against my cheek. I reach up to pet the soft fur and it changes to a beautiful rainbow of colours under my fingers. The alien audience oohs and ahhs as Sploot jumps on my head and moves over to my other shoulder.

"We can show you how to love and make the sploots happy. When they are happy, they will make you happy. The more love you give them, the more beautiful colours they show, and the more they'll love you back. Just give them a chance to be your friend instead of your hat. Come on up here and we'll show you how to love a sploot." All the aliens line up for their turn to love a sploot.

Matt, Celeste, and I are busy showing the three-headed Mayor how to have a sploot sit on her shoulder, so we don't notice V'alvlax and Omega-Grog next in line. V'alvlax stares hard at us as the turntable screeches and music stops. Everyone stops chattering and we all freeze, as we wait to see what he'll do. The mayor breaks the silence.

"V'alvlax, I'm disappointed that you didn't tell us that sploots make better friends than accessories!" She fixes him with a six-eyed death stare.

"Madam Mayors! So nice to see you enjoying the show. Heh-heh. I was just about to tell you how happy I am about this fashion show . . . Errr, I mean, sploot parade."

She gives him a curt nod of her heads. "I certainly hope so. I wouldn't want to take away all *your* trade and business permits here on Furilani. We have intelligent life here. Don't make me deport you to Vo'lox."

"No, please Mayors! I will change our business model immediately to 'Parades-R-Us.' I can see that sploots are talented and intelligent beings. We never should have sold them as merchandise." I notice V'alvlax isn't wearing his sploot belt anymore.

"I hope these talented Earthlings will share their secrets for the Furilani Parade. We're the hit of the galaxy! The multiverse! The parades are sold out for the rest of the millennium!"

Matt, Celeste, Sploot, and I look at each other in disbelief. *What?!*

CHAPTER 17

ALL YOU NEED IS LOVE

Everyone stares at us and waits for an answer. V'alvlax's face quivers impatiently.

"Um, sorry V'alvlax, but we can't stay here for a millennium. That sounds like a long time. We need to go home. Back to Earth, like, soon, or our families will worry about us." I look at Matt and Celeste and they both nod. "We had the parade to show you how funny and intelligent these gentle little sploots are, so that you will respect and love them. They don't want to be your slaves anymore."

V'alvlax looks devastated. "B-b-but we do love the sploots. And we love their shows. Can you ask them to do more parades and basketball games for us? Pleeeeaaase? We want to be the entertainment capital of the galaxy." V'alvlax is on the verge of whining.

I look at Sploot on my shoulder, who nods. "Why don't you ask them yourself?" I point to all the sploots on the float and the railings who watch V'alvlax with big eyes.

V'alvlax looks around and clears his throat. "Ahem. Yes, well, I know that many of you must be angry with me for making you into hats and scarves, and I don't blame you for that. I humbly apologize for what we did. I didn't know that you were so talented and intelligent. Can you please show us how to put on a sploot

parade?" V'alvlax nervously looks down at the ground and waits for the sploots' answer. I can tell that he's worried that the sploots will say no after what they've been through.

But suddenly, hundreds of beautifully coloured sploots rush up onto the float. They've been released from the farm and led back to their family. Sploot wiggles around on my shoulder as hordes of sploots surround the float. V'alvlax is astonished when some of them approach him and rub against his legs and sit down in front of him expectantly. V'alvlax doesn't know what to do. So Sploot and I take his hand and guide him down to the ground. When he sits amongst the beautifully coloured sploots, they take turns jumping on his lap and shoulder and rubbing against his cheek. V'alvlax turns bright red and blushes with pleasure.

"How come they don't hate me?" V'alvlax looks up at Sploot and I. "Why do they like me? I wouldn't like me if I were them." Sploot jumps down onto V'alvlax's shoulder and chitters in his ear. V'alvlax hangs his head down and starts to cry. Tears stream from his six eyes, down his long face, and splash on the sploots' heads in his lap. One little sploot shakes the water off himself like a wet dog after a bath, which makes us all laugh. The funny little sploot looks around and smiles, proud that he lightened everybody's mood. These sploots are natural comedians. They seem to like to entertain and bring happiness into the lives of others. Maybe basketball games, juggling, and rapping are what these sploots want to do? I look at Sploot, who's back on my shoulder, nodding like they've read my mind.

"V'alvlax, the sploots have agreed that they want to do more parades. It makes them happy to make you happy."

"This is exciting news." V'alvlax pets a sploot who lays on their back in front of him.

I put my hand up to stop him. "Wait a second. There are a few conditions. I speak for all sploots when I say that they will keep Splootsville for their home. No one is allowed in Splootsville, except sploots. And they must be respected. The sploots will decide when to participate in the games and parades."

V'alvlax nods as the Mayor approaches the group. "I will make a law that forbids the sale *and* wearing of sploots," she says.

"Yay!" We all cheer and fist-pump. "Whoop whoop!"

V'alvlax looks around at all the sploots on his lap, and he looks a little sad. "I want to invite some of my friends here back to my place for health water and protein logs."

Matt jumps up. "C'mon everyone, dance party at V'alvlax's pad!"

All the sploots turn their heads and strike a pose with a duckface.

CHAPTER 18

THAT'S A RAP

There's a big party at V'alvlax's place with beings from every corner of the galaxy. V'alvlax didn't know what he was getting into, but everyone from the parade and all the spectators came back to his house. It's lucky he has a huge mansion the size of a football field, because the Space-Mart guys brought in Busta-Masta Matt's rap stage. Then the party was really rocking. Matt and his posse rap and dance and teach everyone the chorus so they can sing along. They rap 'Sploots ain't no Bling,' 'Grog in da House,' and the biggest hit of the night, 'The Prism Slide.' The party goes on all night. Beings enjoy themselves and have fun until Matt and his band fall asleep. Celeste and I show V'alvlax and Omega-Grog some breakdancing moves like the 'Bigfoot Challenge,' and the 'Splooty Swag,' and then Grog makes up the 'V'alvlax twitch.' Finally, we know that it's time to say our goodbyes. The hardest one is my Sploot.

Celeste, Matt, Sploot, and I walk out to the rainbow forest. Celeste holds the radio out in front of us, reading the dials. We look for a signal on the tuner to get us back home. I look down and tell Sploot, "This is it, little buddy. I have to go back to Earth and my life."

Sploot hides inside my hoodie, and when I unzip it, they put their paws over their eyes. I don't think Sploot wants to say goodbye. This is harder than I thought.

"I'm really going to miss you," I tell Sploot. "I never had a pet before."

Sploot looks at me with soulful eyes and rubs their head against mine. Sploot makes little crying noises, and my ESP tells me that they don't want me to leave.

"You've given me a special gift that I never thought I would have. You were my friend while I was here, and I'll never forget you." I gently pull Sploot out of my sweater and kiss their soft head. I wipe the tears off my cheeks as I leave Sploot on the side of the road and run to catch up with Matt and Celeste.

Celeste and Matt concentrate on the radio, but I can tell that they are giving me a minute to pull myself together. I rub my eyes and swallow hard. My bottom lip trembles. When I look back, Sploot is gone.

Celeste calls me over. "Here, Hawk. I think we have it." She shows me the radio and I check to make sure that we do the same trip in reverse and go home. I don't feel up to any more planet hopping right now. I didn't know it would hurt so much to leave Sploot behind and never see them again. Gosh, I wish I could take them with us. But I don't want to take them away from their home and family and friends. *I love you Sploot! And I wish I could take you with us.* I think really hard inside my head. Maybe they'll hear me.

Matt, Celeste, and I hold hands as the radio waves encircle us from Matt's backpack, where the radio is safely stowed. We hear the familiar static of the radio connection and the hair on the back of my neck prickles. Green light and electricity flickers and pops all around us as the electromagnetic force pulls us in. We spin in zero gravity down a tunnel that stretches and shrinks, as points of light turn into elongated streaks. That's when I pass out.

I wake up on the floor of Mission Control. I look around at all the posters on the walls and the ugly orange couch, and it feels like time stood still here. I don't move yet. I guess we survived the trip. But I don't even care about that right now. I'm still worried about my Sploot, and how sad they looked all alone at the side of the road. I am mad at myself for feeling this way. Why didn't I ask Sploot to come with us? Maybe they wanted to and I didn't bother to ask. *Oh brother!* What doofus I am. Now I'll never have another chance and we'll never see each other again. I start to weep and I can't stop. Then I feel something weird behind my head. What is that!? Something moved. I sit up because I can hear strange sounds from my hood. What the . . . ?

Sploot jumps out of my hood onto my shoulder and looks at me, waiting for my reaction. Well, I can tell you my reaction was shock!

"Sploot! How did . . . What are you doing here?" My eyes are wide and I start to sob. Happy tears this time. "Oh, come here, Sploot." I hold them and cuddle them to my chest. I'm so happy right now. "How did you know that I wanted to ask you to come home with me?" I look into their big brown eyes and they chitter in my ear. "Oh, you heard what my heart said to you. I knew you were smart, but now I know you're smarter than I am." I hug them again as Sploot wiggles around

me like a rainbow ferret. We laugh and roll around the floor when Matt and Celeste wake up and join us.

"Wait! How did Sploot get here? I feel like I'm still in a time-warp." Matt yawns and collapses next to me.

I laugh as Sploot turns orange like the couch and we can't see him anymore. "Sploot hitched a ride in my hood! Can you believe it?"

I am over the moon happy until Celeste says, "Do you think your mom will let you keep them?"

I hear the turntable in my head screech to a stop as I imagine what mom and dad will say. "Oh no!"

Stay tuned!

GLOSSARY OF SPACE AND SCIENCE TERMS

Andromeda: The closest galaxy to the Milky Way.

Appendages: A body part (such as an arm or leg) that is attached to the main part of the body.

Black hole: A region of space where matter has collapsed in on itself.

Camouflage: To hide yourself by making yourself look like the things around you. Blending in.

Chameleon: A small lizard with the ability to change colour to blend into its surroundings.

Cosmic: Relating to the universe or cosmos.

Darwin, Charles: A 17th century, English naturalist, geologist and entomologist known for his theory of evolution.

Defense-mechanism: A technique humans and animals use to protect themselves from getting hurt.

Dilithium: A fictional crystal on the TV show *Star Trekkers*. A beam of matter and antimatter colliding generates a plasma that is used to power the warp drives that allow their starships to travel faster than light.

ESP: Extra Sensory Perception. The ability to read each other's thoughts.

Galaxy: A system of millions or billions of stars, together with gas and dust, held together by gravity.

Geyser: A hot spring that is underground and erupts, sending jets of water and steam into the air.

Gravity: A force that pulls two objects toward each other.

Hawking, Stephen: A 20-21st century cosmologist and theoretical physicist known for his work with black holes and relativity.

Hipster: Someone who wants to be hip and trendy.

Hyperspace Highway: An extra-dimension of space through which starships can travel faster across the galaxy.

Insufficient funds: Your account does not have enough money to cover what you are buying.

Intergalactic: Being or occurring between galaxies.

Levitation: The raising or lifting of a person or thing by supernatural means.

Membrane: A covering, lining, or layer of tissue.

Metagalaxy: The entire system of galaxies or the universe.

Nonporous: Does not allow liquid or air to pass through it.

Oasis: A fertile place with fresh water in the middle of a desert.

Percentage: A number that tells us how many times out of 100 something occurs.

Pneumatic tube transport: Systems that propel cylindrical containers through networks of tubes by compressed air.

Prism: A clear, triangular piece of glass that can reflect light in a special way, separating all of the colours from white light and creating a rainbow.

Supernova: What happens when a star has reached the end of its life and explodes in a brilliant burst of light.

Technicolor: Bright, intense colours.

Telekinesis: The ability to move objects at a distance by mental power.

Universe: All of time and space and its contents. It is made of millions of stars and planets and enormous clouds of gas, separated by a gigantic space.

Whirlpool galaxy: The first galaxy discovered that is shaped like a spiral and is one of galaxies known as the M51 Group. It can be seen with binoculars or a small telescope.

Wookiee: Chewbacca, a tall hairy humanoid, fictional alien race from the Star Wars franchise.

Wormhole: Passage through space, creating a shortcut through time and space.

HOW YOU CAN HELP ANIMALS IN NEED

- Animals are not clothing. Don't wear real leather or fur coats and garments. Fake furs are just as nice and don't involve farming or trapping furry animals for their skins.
- Want to adopt a pet? Drive past the pet store and go to your nearest animal shelter, or check out all the homeless cats, dogs, and rabbits they post online. They're waiting for you.
- Choose vegan chicken nuggets, tofu hotdogs, and veggie burgers to eat sometimes.
- Never leave stray animals on the street. Get adult help and call animal protection services, the SPCA, or your local animal shelter.
- Raise funds with a lemonade stand or a bake sale and sponsor an animal today. Many large animals are abandoned and need our support. Choose a horse, goat, or llama to help. Check out these websites: AnimalsRahat.com/Sponsor or A Horse Tale Rescue in Hudson, QC at ahtrescue.org/
- Avoid roadside zoos or other places that exploit animals for profit.
- Most of all, love your animal companions and always take good care of them. They'll reward you for it.

ABOUT THE AUTHOR

Ann Birdgenaw is a librarian at an elementary school and always wanted to write a book of her own. She was inspired to write this story by a strange beeping coming from a box in her garage. When COVID-19 hit Canada and everyone was in quarantine or lock down, she had lots of time to imagine being sucked through a wormhole to other planets and what wonderful things she might find there.

Ann lives in Montreal, Quebec, Canada with her family and two morkies: Bilbo and Sheba.

Visit Ann at:
https://www.goodreads.com/author/show/21269547.
Ann_Birdgenaw
https://www.facebook.com/Author-Ann-Birdgenaw
-109480387962145
https://www.amazon.ca/Ann-Birdgenaw/e/B0918TC
RRT/ref=dp_byline_cont_pop_book_1
https://www.annbirdgenaw.wordpress.com

@abirdgenaw on Twitter
@annbirdbooks on Instagram

ABOUT THE ILLUSTRATOR

Noa Ne'eman is a freelance artist & arts teacher based in Montreal. Besides narrative illustrations & cartoons, she creates commissioned art in a variety of styles, with an emphasis on portraiture. Noa also teaches painting & drawing classes around the city at various community centres, and has recently delved into game design. Check out her work here; noaneeman.com

Stay Tuned for more exciting adventures through the Black Hole Radio – Book 6.